THE MYSTERY OF BUTCH CASSIDY AND THE SUNDANCE KID

By Janet Serlin Garber

contemporary perspectives, inc.

This book is distributed by Silver Burdett Company, Morristown, New Jersey 07960.

Library of Congress Number: 79-17622

Art and Photo Credits

Cover photos courtesy of Pinkerton's, Inc.
Illustrations on pages 7, 8, 9, 10, 13, 17, 21, 32, 34, 36, 37, 38, 39, 41, 43, 45, 47, 48,
   Mere Images, Inc. Reprinted courtesy of Coronet Instructional Media, a division
   of Esquire, Inc.
Photos on pages 5 and 29, Denver Public Library, Western History Department
Photo on page 15, Wyoming State Archives, Museums and Historical Department
Photos on pages 19, 25, 27, and 31, courtesy of Pinkerton's, Inc.
Every effort has been made to trace the ownership of all copyrighted material in this
book and to obtain permission for its use.

Library of Congress Cataloging in Publication Data

Garber, Janet Serlin.
   The mystery of Butch Cassidy and the Sundance Kid.

   SUMMARY: Relates the exploits of the famous
outlaws Butch Cassidy and the Sundance Kid and
discusses the yet-unsolved mystery of their last days.
   1. Cassidy, Butch, b. 1866 or 7 — Juvenile
literature.2. Sundance Kid — Juvenile literature. 3.
Crime and criminals — The West — History — Juvenile
literature. 4. The West — History — 1848-1950 —
Juvenile literature. 5. Outlaws — The West —
Biography — Juvenile literature. [1. Cassidy, Butch, b.
1866 or 7. 2. Sundance Kid. 3. Robbers and outlaws. 4.
The West — Biography] I. Title.
F595.C362G37   364.1'55'0924   [B]   [920]   79-17622
ISBN 0-89547-075-6

Manufactured in the United States of America
ISBN 0-89547-075-6

Contents

Chapter 1

A Perfect Plan

Telluride was a quiet little town in Col____ ____ st of the time nothing very exciting ever happened there. But one warm summer day in 1889 the town of Telluride became more than just a name on a map.

It was June 24, 1889, and a daring robbery was about to take place. Across the street from the local bank a stranger leaned comfortably against a broken wagon wheel. He seemed to be waiting for something. His name was Robert LeRoy Parker.

No one in Telluride thought very much about Mr. Parker that day. He would not be known by his real name much longer. But people all over the world would talk about him for the next 100 years. One day he would be known as one of the most famous outlaws of all time — Butch Cassidy.

Telluride, Colorado was a sleepy mountain town when Butch Cassidy visited the bank there in the late 1800s.

Butch stood there for a long time. He really didn't mind. What he was waiting for was worth it. If he stayed calm, everything would work out. Butch Cassidy had a plan that couldn't fail.

Finally, the bank's head teller walked out the door. He turned down the street and headed home for lunch. Butch had watched him do this same thing every day for weeks. But today Butch would make his move. Butch suddenly pushed back his hat. He stretched his arms skyward. That was the signal to put his plan into action.

Butch walked slowly across the street. He entered the bank as matter-of-factly as any customer. Inside the bank, only a very young clerk was on hand. Cassidy showed him a check. But when the clerk leaned over to read it, Butch grabbed him around the neck. The young man was scared to death. He closed his eyes and raised his hands above his head. Butch Cassidy didn't have to say a word.

By now two of Cassidy's sidekicks had entered the bank — one through the back door and one through the front. While Butch held the clerk and watched the street from a window, the two scooped up all the gold and money they could find. It came to almost $25,000. They quickly stuffed it into the cloth bags they were carrying. When they had all the money, they ran for the door. Butch told the clerk to lie down on the floor. The poor man was so stunned that they didn't have to tie him up. Butch knew the frightened man would not move an inch until the head teller returned.

When Butch left the bank, his partners were already

on their horses. They wanted to get going — *fast*! But not Butch Cassidy. He took his time. Everything went as planned. No one knew about the holdup yet. Cassidy wanted to keep it that way. Riding wildly out of town would only make folks wonder who they were. Instead, Butch acted as though he was taking a quiet

7

Part of Butch's plan was to ride slowly out of town and not attract any attention.

walk about town. He even tipped his hat to a group of ladies coming out of the nearby general store.

At the very edge of town, Butch stopped for a moment and turned his horse around. His partners kept going, but Butch wanted to take one last look. He had always liked the town of Telluride. It seemed like a nice place to settle down, do some ranching, perhaps raise a family. He had dreamed this way before, about other towns. The dreams never seemed to come true. Things didn't work out. Butch sighed and dug his spurs into his horse. He galloped after his partners. This was not the moment to think about the happiness an honest living might bring him.

Time was short. To make the most of it, they would have to ride their horses hard. Soon the sheriff would get word that the bank had been robbed. Butch knew he could count on no more than a 15-minute head start on the sheriff and his posse.

Soon they reached the point where rested horses were waiting — another step that Butch had planned. Now they could ride even further ahead of the sheriff. The posse had no way to change horses, and the ones they were riding would be too tired to keep up. Cassidy's partners started to laugh. It was not hard for Butch to read their minds. *Everything had gone just as he had said it would. Butch Cassidy's plan was perfect.*

Rested horses waited for Butch and his men just outside the town. That was how they outran the law for years.

Now Butch had another idea. Before riding on, he found some long, dead branches. He tied the branches to one of the tired horses. Then he pointed the horse in the direction of the sheriff. Butch shot a bullet into the air. The horse with the tree branches jumped a

foot off the ground and ran off toward the posse. It looked like a tree that was somehow racing across the open plain, kicking up dust every which way.

Now Butch started laughing. He only wished he could see that sheriff's face when this horse ran crazily past him. Butch was sure the posse's horses would get scared, and the sheriff would give up and head back to town.

Butch happily slapped his partners' backs. They rode off toward the orange sun that was just setting behind the Rocky Mountains. They joked and laughed about the holdup, telling each other the story over and over again. His partners were most pleased with the way Butch had spooked that horse.

Butch Cassidy was pleased too. They had pulled it off and no one had been hurt. But later, when they camped for the night, Butch had some second thoughts. Lying under a clear, star-filled sky, he asked himself some questions. How long could he go on trying to outsmart the law? Did he really want to be the best outlaw in the West? If he had the chance, what kind of life would he really want?

Butch lay back against his saddle. The others were already asleep as he stared up at the stars. Now that he was an outlaw, Butch wondered, would he ever have that ranch and family?

Chapter 2

The Sundance Kid

Butch Cassidy stayed one step ahead of the law for the next few months. He split from the two men who helped rob the Telluride bank. Butch needed to move fast. It would be easier riding alone until he reached Wyoming. He would be safe there for a while. He knew the perfect place to hide. It was the Hole-in-the-Wall — a beautiful valley hidden in the middle of a ring of tall mountains. Butch Cassidy arrived at the Hole-in-the-Wall in 1890.

One side of the Hole-in-the-Wall is called the Red Wall. It is a long line of stone that runs for nearly 50 miles. There are only two openings in the entire wall. Anyone coming into the valley is quickly seen. This made it easy for the men who lived there to hide. With

Butch met the Sundance Kid at the Hole-in-the-Wall, a gangster's hideout in Wyoming. They became lifelong friends.

nature on their side, just a few of them could keep out a lot of lawmen.

Outlaws from all over the West knew the Hole-in-the-Wall. They ran there whenever the law was getting too close. One day, late in the summer of 1892, one such outlaw came to the Hole-in-the-Wall. He was called the Sundance Kid, and he and Butch Cassidy became friends right from the start. It had been three long years since Cassidy had robbed the Telluride bank, and life was lonely.

"Tell me," Sundance asked Butch, soon after they

met, "are all those stories about you true? Are you really as good a shot as they say? I hear you can ride a horse around a tree at full speed and empty every bullet in your gun into a three-inch circle."

Cassidy smiled. "Yep, guess I can," he said. "But that's just for show. I never hurt no one with a gun in my life. Don't intend to either. Robbin' a bank means nothin' to me, but killing is something I don't approve of. I'd rather outwit 'em than kill 'em!"

"I guess so," said Sundance. "Though I'm pretty good with a six-shooter myself. And I can handle just about anything. But that job you pulled in Colorado — now that was really something. The whole town's still tryin' to figure out what happened. How'd you pull it off so smoothly?"

"Aw, wasn't much to it," said the modest Cassidy. "Good planning's the key. And good friends. A man has to have friends he can trust."

Sundance liked what he heard.

"I know what you mean about plannin' and friends," he said. "Do you think your plan would work again?"

Butch thought it over.

"Don't really see why not," he said slowly. "But I. . . ."

Butch Cassidy lived in this cabin while he stayed at the Hole-in-the-Wall.

Sundance had another question.

"Why'd you choose Telluride anyway? Not much of a town."

"I used to work around there," Butch answered. He was happy Sundance had not asked him more about his Telluride plan. "I hauled ore from the mines to the mill, so I knew the area pretty well. As a matter of fact, I ran into some trouble there once."

15

Now Sundance was even more interested in what Butch had to say. He wanted the whole story.

"A rancher there claimed I stole one of his colts," Butch told him. "It was a lie. I'm not the kind of guy who steals *horses*! The colt was mine. It even had my brand." Butch scratched the mark in the dust with his finger: ⊐⊏. "I'd brought that colt all the way from Utah — that's where I'm from. But the rancher had me jailed. Of course, I was cleared of the charges. But I never forgot what happened to me down there."

"Don't blame you," said Sundance. "No one likes to be thrown in jail — 'specially when he ain't done nothing wrong. Was that why you picked Telluride for your first big job?"

"Guess it had something to do with it," Butch answered quietly.

Sundance looked hard at Butch. He had something on his mind, and Butch knew what it was. Before Sundance could say anything, Butch Cassidy spoke again.

"Listen, Sundance, I know what you're thinkin'. That was a good plan in Telluride. Someday I may use it again. But only if things don't work out for me. You see, I'm trying to go straight. After the holdup, I took my share of the money and started ranching with a friend — Al Hainer.

"We got ourselves a spread outside Lander,
Wyoming. It's a beautiful place to settle down. I have a
lot of friends there too. Even a lady, name of Mary
Boyd. Some day, if everything quiets down, maybe
the law won't care about me anymore. Then, me and
Mary might just . . . ."

Sundance looked surprised. "Didn't know you went
straight," he said. "But then what are you doing here
in the Hole-in-the-Wall? Didn't you care for ranching?"

"I liked it well enough, and I had enough money to get started." Butch sighed. "But ranching just didn't seem to like me. The weather was against us the first winter. And in the spring it was the larger ranchers. They got together and wouldn't let us smaller guys take part in rounding up stray cattle. They wanted everything for themselves. And the lawmen didn't help. They were always coming around looking for me. Anyway, my money finally ran out. So these days I do my ranching here in the Hole-in-the-Wall. How 'bout yourself?"

"Oh," said Sundance. "I'm here resting up from a little robbery some boys and I pulled over in Montana. Two fellows got caught. But they couldn't get me. Now that I'm here, don't know what I'll be doin'."

Butch invited Sundance to share a meal. Over some stew and coffee, they talked more about themselves.

Butch Cassidy said that his real name was Robert LeRoy Parker. He was born in 1866 in Utah. When he was 18 he changed his name and left home. He took the name of the cowboy who taught him how to ride and shoot. This fellow also taught him what he knew about the art of cattle rustling. For a time Cassidy worked as a butcher. It was then that he picked up the "Butch" part of his name. Robert Parker took on the name Butch Cassidy so he wouldn't disgrace his family.

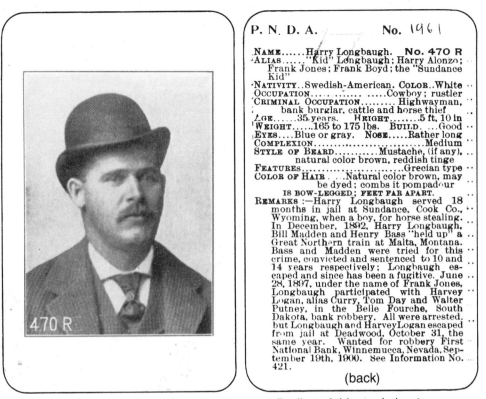

P. N. D. A. .... No. 1961

NAME......Harry Longbaugh. No. 470 R
ALIAS......"Kid" Longbaugh; Harry Alonzo;
   Frank Jones; Frank Boyd; the "Sundance
   Kid"
NATIVITY..Swedish-American. COLOR..White
   OCCUPATION........... .....Cowboy; rustler
CRIMINAL OCCUPATION......... Highwayman,
   bank burglar, cattle and horse thief
AGE......35 years. HEIGHT........5 ft, 10 in
WEIGHT......165 to 175 lbs. BUILD. ...Good
EYES....Blue or gray. NOSE.....Rather long
COMPLEXION.........................Medium
STYLE OF BEARD..........Mustache, (if any),
   natural color brown, reddish tinge
FEATURES..........................Grecian type
COLOR OF HAIR....Natural color brown, may
   be dyed; combs it pompadour
IS BOW-LEGGED; FEET FAR APART.
REMARKS :—Harry Longbaugh served 18
   months in jail at Sundance, Cook Co.,
   Wyoming, when a boy, for horse stealing.
   In December, 1892, Harry Longbaugh,
   Bill Madden and Henry Bass "held up" a
   Great Northern train at Malta, Montana.
   Bass and Madden were tried for this
   crime, convicted and sentenced to 10 and
   14 years respectively; Longbaugh es-
   caped and since has been a fugitive. June
   28, 1897, under the name of Frank Jones,
   Longbaugh participated with Harvey
   Logan, alias Curry, Tom Day and Walter
   Putney, in the Belle Fourche, South
   Dakota, bank robbery. All were arrested,
   but Longbaugh and Harvey Logan escaped
   from jail at Deadwood, October 31, the
   same year. Wanted for robbery First
   National Bank, Winnemucca, Nevada, Sep-
   tember 19th, 1900. See Information No.
   421.

(back)

Pinkerton's National Detective Agency distributed this card about the Sundance Kid.

The Sundance Kid was born Harry Longabaugh in the early 1860s. His family was from Pennsylvania. He came west around 1886 because he wanted to find work as a cowboy. But Harry was caught horse stealing. He'd picked up his nickname after spending 18 months in a jail in Sundance, Wyoming.

After supper Butch and Sundance said goodbye. It had been the start of a great friendship. Both men knew it. They said they would see each other again. But for now each man had to go his own way.

Chapter 3

The Wild Bunch Gang

After three years in the Hole-in-the-Wall, Butch Cassidy decided it was time for a change. He missed his friends in Wyoming, especially Mary Boyd. He still wanted to go straight more than anything. He thought things might have quieted down enough by now for him to give it another try.

Butch and his old partner, Al Hainer, bought two horses from a friend of Al's. They set out for Lander, Wyoming. It was a perfect day to start a new life. The sun shone brightly in the clear sky, and a soft breeze kept them cool.

Everything was looking up until they reached Lander. A welcoming committee was waiting for them on the outskirts of town.

"Cassidy? Hainer?" barked the sheriff, who sat
straight on his horse. There were six men behind him.

"Yeah?" answered Butch, looking questioningly at
Hainer.

"You're under arrest!"

"What in blazes for?" demanded Butch.

"Horse stealin'," said the sheriff.

"You must be kidding," answered the stunned Cassidy.

"We're not kidding," said the sheriff, and he proved it
by pointing the muzzle of his six-shooter directly at Butch.

21

"These are *our* horses. We bought 'em yesterday. What was that fellow's name?" Butch asked Al.

"Never mind the names," said the sheriff. "Just show me a bill of sale, and I'll forget the whole thing."

Butch felt a sinking feeling in the pit of his stomach. He had suspected that the horses he bought from Al's "friend" had been stolen, but he'd been in a hurry and Al trusted the man. So he didn't get a bill of sale. Now it looked as if Butch and Al had stolen the horses.

"O.K.," continued the sheriff, "put your hands up and come with me."

The sheriff brought both Butch and Al into Lander, where the two men stood trial. Strangely, Al was found not guilty, while Butch received a two-year prison sentence at hard labor. Butch knew that Al had double-crossed him so he could get off free. But Butch never held it against him. Nor did he ever seek revenge.

Butch served his sentence as a model prisoner, and he was finally released in 1896. The first thing he wanted to do was "go straight" — get a regular job on a ranch. But the big ranchers didn't trust him because of his reputation as an outlaw. Hard as he tried, he couldn't find work as a hired hand. Butch finally gave up trying.

"I can't make it," he told his friends. "No one will hire me. They're forcing me back into a life of crime. I guess they *want* me to be an outlaw!"

"Nobody can force you to become an outlaw," argued Mary Boyd, Butch's sweetheart. "Why can't we move? We could start fresh in another part of the country. There's always a way."

But Butch didn't see it that way. "If they force me into being an outlaw, well, I'm going to be the best and most feared outlaw in the country! I'm going back to the Hole-in-the-Wall," he decided. "That's the only real home I've ever had!"

Back at the Hole-in-the-Wall, Butch rounded up the toughest bunch of criminals he could find. It wasn't difficult. It seemed as if they were all waiting for someone to tell them what to do. Butch became their leader. And his right-hand man was his old friend Harry Longabaugh — the Sundance Kid.

"This time," Butch told Sundance, "if I'm going back to jail, it's going to be for something I really did — and it's going to be for something big!"

Between 1896 and 1901, Butch's gang stole almost $300,000 in eight major robberies. They were hunted by lawmen in eight different states. Soon everyone in the country was on the lookout for the horseback gang that came to be called the Wild Bunch.

Under Butch's leadership they always managed to stay one step ahead of the law. Butch kept everyone guessing. Not even members of his own gang could predict what he would do next. He kept changing his habits: he would walk differently, wear different clothes, and change his hairstyle. He used a lot of different names. And the law never caught up with him.

Butch and his gang became the most famous outlaws in the country — feared, hunted, but never caught. They were known as "gentlemen" bandits because they never killed anyone if they could help it. Butch Cassidy liked to stay out of that kind of trouble, not out of fear but out of what he called "policy."

Most of their success was due to Butch's careful planning — and daring. They outran the law for so long because Butch had perfected the getaway plan that he had used in that first robbery in Telluride, Colorado.

Butch developed a system of "relay" horses. He and a few men would pull off a train holdup or a bank job and then ride out of town on horses specially trained by Butch to ride fast and hard. At a preplanned location, Butch would have trusted friends waiting with fresh thoroughbreds — the fastest-running

Pinkerton's card about Butch Cassidy. These cards helped Pinkerton's detectives identify and capture outlaws, who often changed their names and appearances.

horses in the world. When the two groups met, they would either switch horses and split up or set the tired horses free to wander where they would. Any posse that had not given up when the horses tired would now become hopelessly confused about which trail to follow.

Butch's use of the finest, fastest horses and his careful planning became his trademarks.

Chapter 4

Trying to Go Straight

In 1901, Butch Cassidy was 35, and he had been an outlaw for 12 years. He and his gang were the most famous bandits in the country. They knew what it was like to run and hide and be chased every day of their lives. Butch was such a "wanted" man that one mistake would mean his life.

He hid in Los Angeles, Chicago, Texas, and Michigan — any place where people were not likely to recognize him. Once in a great while, he would sneak back to Lander, Wyoming to see Mary and his friends. But for the most part he was always on the run.

Butch never liked the outlaw life. So one day, in another effort to go straight, he went to see a criminal lawyer and judge in Salt Lake City.

The Wild Bunch, called "gentlemen bandits," became the most famous and feared outlaws of their time.

"I want to go straight," he told them. "Can you arrange it with the governor? Maybe you can get him to agree to pardon me for the things they say I've done."

"Well," said the judge. "This is a strange offer. But I'll see what I can do."

"Just try. That's all I ask."

The judge set up a meeting with the governor. "I'm impressed with your offer," said the governor. "Do you really mean what you say?"

"Of course I do," answered Butch. "I want to be a free man. I'll try anything."

"Well, I can't pardon you for the things that happened in other states, but I will suggest this. If the Union Pacific Railroad is willing to drop their charges against you, will you offer your services as a railway guard? I'm sure they could use someone with your, uh, experience."

"Sure," smiled Butch. "I told you, I've wanted to go straight all my life. All I want is a chance."

Butch was to meet the railroad officials and close the deal. He always had to be careful of a double-cross, so the meeting was set up in an out-of-the-way place. Butch showed up alone. He waited, but the railroad men never arrived. Butch was angry. He felt cheated. He left them a note telling them how unfairly everybody had always treated him.

And just to make sure they got the message, Butch and the Wild Bunch held up another train.

Once again, they were on the run. This time, instead of hiding in the wilderness and rugged mountains of the West, Butch, Sundance, and Sundance's girlfriend, Etta Place, headed for New York City.

The Wild Bunch dynamited and robbed so many Union Pacific Railroad cars that a special reward was offered by the railway for the gang's capture.

From there, they decided to sail to Argentina. They had plenty of money from their last holdup and with it they could buy a ranch and stop running from the law.

"Life will be beautiful for the first time," announced Butch to his two friends. "No more worries. No more being chased around. Peace and quiet at last."

Soon after they arrived in South America, they bought a ranch in Cholilo, Argentina and started living a normal life. They even used their real names, Robert Parker and Harry Longabaugh. Etta was known as

Señora Longabaugh. They were honest ranchers and their neighbors liked them. They were finally happy.

The peace and quiet lasted only three years. One day in 1905 they were spotted by an old sheriff from Wyoming. He had gone to Argentina to buy cattle, and he recognized Butch and the Sundance Kid immediately. He went to the police and told them there was a big reward for the outlaws — dead or alive — in the United States.

The police charged up to the Cholilo ranch.

"Give yourselves up," they called out, "and nobody will be hurt."

"Give ourselves up?" Butch laughed. "Never! We haven't done anything here to break the law."

Then Butch and Sundance put on an amazing display of marksmanship. They threw rocks into the air and split them with bullets above the policemen's heads. The police got the message and left the ranch in a big hurry.

But the damage was done. They had been discovered in South America, and once again the chase was on. Butch, Sundance, and Etta returned to what they knew best — robbing banks and holding up

This picture was taken of the Sundance Kid and Etta Place in New York City, just before they sailed for South America.

Not long after arriving in South America, Butch and the Sundance Kid went back to their old ways — robbing banks and trains.

trains. Soon they were known all over Argentina as the "Bandidos Yanquís," and they were right back where they started.

This time they ran to neighboring Bolivia. From time to time they would take jobs, but the jobs wouldn't last very long. Finally Etta decided to return to the United States. Sundance gave her all his money. Maybe the life they were leading became too hard for her. Or maybe she worried about where it would all lead.

In any event, there are no further records of Etta Place. We don't know what she did next. And exactly what happened to Butch and Sundance is also a mystery.

Chapter 5

Did It End in South America  ?

In 1930 an article by a Western historian named Arthur Chapman appeared in *Elks Magazine*. It told a story of the last days of Butch Cassidy and the Sundance Kid.

According to the story, Butch and Sundance rode up to a local Bolivian inn one afternoon for a meal. They were riding two mules they had stolen the week before from a payroll team they had held up in the mountains. They tied the mules up outside the inn and went in for dinner.

While they were eating, one of the villagers noticed the brand on the mules as belonging to the mine that

Once again, Butch and Sundance were wanted men.

had been held up. He ran to the local police station and described Butch and Sundance as the men who had ridden up on the mules.

The policeman realized that the men he was hearing about were the feared Bandidos Yanquís. There was a large reward offered for their capture. The policeman notified the captain of a Bolivian cavalry troop that was stationed in the village, and then he ran over to the inn to arrest the men.

"Surrender, señores," he called as he neared the inn.

But before anything more was said, Cassidy leaped to his feet and shot him. The policeman staggered out to the courtyard and fell. Cassidy and Sundance ran to the window and door of the inn where they had a better view of the square. The Bolivian troops were arriving and a shootout began. First the captain of the troops ran toward the inn. Before he got halfway there, Sundance shot from the hip and he fell. Two of the captain's men then rushed to help him. They also fell.

Butch squinted out into the sunny courtyard. The captain's troops were lining up around the square. Butch scanned the roads leading away from the village and saw more army men on horseback standing there. Sundance was also surveying the area, wondering how they could steal some horses and make their escape.

"Butch, I think they have the whole army out after us!" said Sundance, amazed.

At that moment some cavalry men rushed the inn.

"Surrender, bandidos! We know who you are!"

Bullets whistled through the air. Horses kicked up dust. Cassidy and Sundance were shooting fast but carefully. They had two six-shooters each, but most of their ammunition and their rifles had been left on the mules.

The cavalry troops shot wildly. Bullets sank into the
walls of the inn. Butch and Sundance were
outnumbered, but they were in a better position
behind the walls of the inn. No one dared approach
them. Anyone who did was killed immediately.
Sundance never missed a shot. But they were running
out of bullets.

"Keep me covered, Butch," yelled Sundance. "I'm
going to make a run for our rifles."

Sundance burst from the inn, shooting as he went.
Sundance thought he had only to sprint to where the

mules were tied up. But when he ran outside he saw that the mules had broken their harnesses and galloped away. Guns were blazing all around. Sundance got about halfway back to the inn when he fell, wounded.

Butch cursed in anger. He rushed out as bullets flew. He dragged Sundance to safety and then lifted him up and staggered back to the inn. Just before he crawled to safety, he too was hit.

"Butch, we'll never get out of here alive," whispered Sundance.

Night fell around the courtyard and fewer and fewer shots were fired from the inn. Still, no one dared enter the firing range of the two famous outlaws. Finally, two shots rang out. The remaining cavalry men feared it was a trick to lure them into the inn. They continued firing from a distance all through the night.

The next morning a group of soldiers rushed into the inn. According to Chapman's story, they found Butch

and Sundance dead. Butch had shot the seriously
wounded Sundance Kid and then, with his last bullet,
shot himself.

Chapman's story was picked up by the press and in
the April 23, 1930, edition of the *Washington Post*
the story appeared under the banner headline
"BUTCH IS DEAD."

But was he?

Twenty years later, a man named William T. Phillips said he knew better. He claimed his real name was Robert Parker and that he was the famous Butch Cassidy.

Phillips said there never was a shootout in Bolivia. It was just an imaginary story. In 1935 Phillips wrote a book called *The Bandit Invincible, the Story of Butch Cassidy.* In it, he tells what he says is the true story.

In Phillips's story, Butch and Sundance were hiding in the mountains at the time they were supposedly in the shootout with the Bolivian army in San Vicente. They were planning to hold up another pack train of mules coming from the mines with a payroll. They had two friends with them.

Cassidy, Sundance, and one of their friends carefully placed themselves along the mountain trail. They listened for the tinkle of the bells on the mules that led the payroll pack up the mountain. Their other friend stayed farther up the mountain with the horses. Around three o'clock, the payroll team rounded the curve.

"Hands up all of you, and quick!" yelled Cassidy.

The riders obeyed. They put their hands above their heads and Sundance took away their guns. Cassidy

Phillips claimed to tell the true story of Butch Cassidy's life in his book *The Bandit Invincible, the Story of Butch Cassidy*.

began gathering the loot. Suddenly, Bolivian soldiers rounded the curve and started shooting.

Butch and Sundance raced to safety behind some rocks. The man they had left behind with the horses was the first to get killed. Then their other friend was shot. There were many soldiers, and Butch and Sundance were badly outnumbered. But they had good cover behind boulders, and no one dared approach them because they were such deadly shots.

Bullets blazed and Sundance was hit. Phillips says he tried to help Sundance, but there was nothing he could do except make Sundance as comfortable as possible. Butch then tried to think of a way to escape. He crawled through the bushes for hours until he reached the horses. Luckily, they were still there. Then he rode up the mountain under cover of darkness and got away.

Butch rode for days until he reached Brazil. It was a long, hard trip, but no one had followed him. He realized then that he had lost a small packet of letters and clippings that he always had with him. He must have left it back in the mountains where he left his friends. The packet would be found with the three men and everyone would think that Butch had died with them. Butch was happy to let them think that.

From Brazil, Phillips says he booked passage on a ship to England. From there he went to Paris and checked into a hospital. Three weeks later, he had a new face! The doctors had changed his identity. Cassidy took on the name Phillips and sailed home to the United States — a new man.

Phillips's story is very interesting. But is it true? Why should we believe his story and not Arthur Chapman's? A look at the rest of Phillips's life may have some clues.

According to Phillips's story, Butch Cassidy returned to America with a
new identity.

Chapter 6

A Stranger Named William T. Phillips

In 1908, the same year Butch Cassidy was said to have been killed, Phillips visited Adrian, Michigan. This is the first official record we have of him. Phillips quickly made a lot of friends, and in May he married a local woman. At the wedding, Phillips said he was from Des Moines, Iowa, and that he was 34 years old. Butch Cassidy would have been 42, but that does not mean we cannot believe his story.

Phillips and his wife then moved out West. He worked as a ranch hand and on construction crews. For a short time he rode as a sharp-shooter in Pancho Villa's army. They were fighting against the Mexican government.

In 1910, Phillips and his wife moved to the state of Washington. On their way, they stopped for a while in Lander, Wyoming. Phillips told his wife that he wanted to visit some old friends. Many years later, these people said they recognized him as the famous outlaw Butch Cassidy!

The fact is, there are several important people in Cassidy's life who agree that Phillips was telling the truth. One is his sister, who lives in Utah.

William T. Phillips visited Butch Cassidy's sister in Lander, Wyoming. She was one of many people who believed that Phillips was really Butch Cassidy.

"The law thought he was dead," she said in 1970. "And he was happy to leave it that way. He made us promise not to tell anyone he was alive. And we never did. It was the closest family secret. I tell you Butch Cassidy did not die somewhere in Bolivia. My brother died in Spokane, Washington in 1937."

Mary Boyd, Butch's old girlfriend, also believed Phillips was Cassidy. She met him again near the end of his life, and says he remembered things about the times they spent together that only Butch could have known.

Today, Phillips has a granddaughter. She has a ring that Butch gave Mary many years ago. Inside the ring are their initials. Phillips's granddaughter also has some letters that Phillips wrote to Mary from Spokane. A handwriting expert has compared them with a signature believed to be Butch Cassidy's. He is convinced they were all written by the same person.

There is more evidence that Phillips is telling the truth. Before he died, he gave a friend in Spokane a set of hand guns. Carved into the grip of one of the guns is Butch's famous brand: ⊒⊏ . But the most interesting thing about Phillips is how he lived, and how similar his life was to Cassidy's.

Phillips tried to settle down and live a normal life many times. But somehow he kept moving from place

Phillips's granddaughter has a ring, letters, and a pistol that could have only belonged to Butch.

to place. In Spokane, Washington he worked for a while for the Water Power Company. Then he tried to start his own business making and inventing machine parts. In 1912, he went gold hunting in Alaska, but he was forced to return empty-handed.

Phillips and his wife then adopted a son. For a while his life was very pleasant. People who knew him then liked him. And they remember that he was a good shot and excellent horseman.

But in 1925, Phillips left his family to take another trip. First he went to Utah to visit his sister. And then he went to Wyoming. People say he was there to look

Phillips was a restless man. In his later years, he traveled to many of Butch Cassidy's old haunts.

for some of the loot he and the Wild Bunch gang had buried there during his outlaw days. Phillips traveled along the old Union Pacific Railroad line digging up many holes. But again he found nothing. When he went back to Spokane, he wrote the book about his life. He died there several years later in 1937.

Was William T. Phillips really Butch Cassidy? Perhaps it will remain a mystery no one will ever solve. But even if they were the same man, it seems neither one ever did find the peace and quiet he was looking for. Even after he changed his identity, Phillips appears to have spent his life running from place to place and hiding from his past. Both Phillips and Cassidy were restless men. And things never seemed to work out quite the way they planned.